I0662786

The Beast in the Cave

Lovecraft's Classic Horror Story –
Lost and Hunted Underground

A Modern Translation

Adapted for the Contemporary Reader

H.P. Lovecraft

Translated by Tim Zengerink

Table of Contents

Preface - Message to the Reader

What If You Could Help Rebuild the Greatest Library in Human History?

Thousands of years ago, the Library of Alexandria stood as the crown jewel of human achievement — a sanctuary where the collected wisdom of every known civilization was gathered, preserved, and shared freely.

And then, it was lost.

Through fire, conquest, and the slow erosion of time, humanity lost not just books — but ideas, dreams, discoveries, and stories that could have changed the world forever.

Today, the Library of Alexandria lives again — and you are invited to be a part of its restoration.

Our mission is simple yet profound:

To rebuild the greatest library the world has ever known, and to translate all timeless works into every language and dialect, so that no seeker of knowledge is ever left behind again.

By joining our movement to rebuild the modern Library of Alexandria, you become part of an unprecedented mission:

- **Unlimited Access to the Greatest Audiobooks & eBooks Ever Written:**

  Instantly explore thousands of legendary works—Plato, Shakespeare, Jane Austen, Leo Tolstoy, and countless more. All instantly available to read or listen, placing a complete literary universe at your fingertips.

- **Beautiful Paperback & Deluxe Editions at Printing Cost**

  Own any title as an elegant paperback, deluxe hardcover, or stunning collectible boxset—offered to you at true printing cost, delivered straight to your door. Build your personal Library of Alexandria, crafted for beauty, built for durability, and worthy of proud display.

- **Fresh Translations for Modern Readers—in Every Language & Dialect**

  Enjoy timeless masterpieces reimagined in clear, contemporary language—no more outdated phrases or obscure references. Alongside the original versions, we're tirelessly translating these classics into every language and dialect imaginable, ensuring accessibility and understanding across cultures and generations.

- **Join a Global Renaissance of Literature & Knowledge**

  You directly support expanding our library, publishing deluxe editions at true cost, translating works into all global languages, and bringing humanity's greatest stories to people everywhere. By joining today, you're not just preserving a legacy of masterpieces; you set in motion a powerful wave of literary accessibility.

Become a Torchbearer of Knowledge.

Join us for free now at **LibraryofAlexandria.com**

Together, we will ensure that the light of human wisdom never fades again.

With gratitude and a shared love of knowledge,

The Modern Library of Alexandria Team

Visit:

www.libraryofalexandria.com

Or scan the code below:

Introduction

Darkness, Dehumanization, and the Limits of Perception

H.P. Lovecraft's "The Beast in the Cave," written when he was just fourteen years old and first published in 1918, is often treated as a juvenile curiosity, a formative sketch of the ideas he would later develop into the vast and terrifying architecture of the Cthulhu Mythos. But to dismiss the story as merely apprentice work is to overlook its core significance: even in this early effort, Lovecraft displays a precocious grasp of his favorite themes—namely, the limits of human understanding, the horror of degeneration, and the existential terror that emerges when identity itself begins to dissolve. "The Beast in the Cave" is a compact, elegant fable that uses a simple premise to devastating effect: what if the monsters we fear are not only real, but once were just like us?

The story follows an unnamed narrator who becomes separated from a tour group during an excursion through a vast subterranean cavern system. At first confident in his ability to find his way back, the

5

narrator gradually becomes overwhelmed by the impenetrable darkness and the eerie silence that envelops him. Panic sets in as he realizes he may be lost forever, consigned to die slowly in the black belly of the earth. But as he resigns himself to despair, he hears something—footsteps. At first hopeful that it is his .guide, he soon realizes that the sound is unnatural, shuffling, and hesitant. It is not a rescuer. It is something else. Something alive. Something watching him from the dark.

In an act of primal fear, the narrator hurls a stone at the oncoming presence, striking it down. When a search party eventually finds him, they examine the fallen creature with lantern light—and discover to their horror that the beast is no animal, no alien thing, but a man. Or rather, what remains of a man. Pale, eyeless, and grotesquely deformed from a life lived in total darkness, it is a human being reduced to something less than human—a warning of what the narrator himself might have become, had he remained in the cave long enough.

This final revelation transforms the story from a tale of external menace to one of internal dread. The beast is not the other—it is the self, altered by time, environment, and deprivation. Lovecraft suggests that the line between man and monster is terrifyingly thin, and that the true horror lies not in what lurks outside, but in what we are capable of becoming under the right (or wrong) conditions. Even at fourteen, Lovecraft was exploring one of the fundamental questions of horror literature: What is it, really, that separates us from the abyss?

Though short and formally straightforward, "The Beast in the Cave" is saturated with metaphysical dread. The cave becomes a symbol of more than just physical entrapment. It is a space of unknowing, a metaphor for the unconscious mind, the blind spot of civilization, the realm where history and progress do not reach. In this space, the structures of reason and morality begin to erode. The narrator's descent into panic is not simply a reaction to being lost—it is the collapse of identity when severed from light, time, and companionship. The beast, then, is not a creature. It is a future. A possibility. A fate.

Subterranean Symbolism and the Psychological Architecture of Fear

Caves have always held a unique place in the human imagination. They are sites of birth and burial, initiation and revelation. From Plato's allegory of the cave to the myth of the Minotaur's labyrinth, underground spaces serve as metaphors for the unknown depths of the mind and the unseen forces of nature. In Lovecraft's hands, the cave in this story becomes a crucible of transformation—a place where the self confronts its own fragility and where the illusion of control gives way to raw, elemental fear.

What makes this story stand out, even among Lovecraft's mature works, is its economy. With just a few thousand words, Lovecraft conjures an entire philosophy of horror. The slow build-up of dread, the oppressive atmosphere, the psychological realism of the narrator's descent into fear—it all works seamlessly to create a profound emotional impact. There are no supernatural elements, no forbidden books, no ancient cults. The horror here is entirely natural, which makes it all the more terrifying. The beast is not summoned. It is not cursed. It is not evil. It is simply a man who, in losing the light, lost everything else.

This naturalistic approach anticipates Lovecraft's later rejection of traditional Gothic horror in favor of what he called "cosmic indifference." While this early story does not yet explore extraterrestrial or extradimensional threats, it already embraces the idea that the universe is not governed by human morality, and that nature, when left to itself, will not preserve our sanity, dignity, or form. In "The Beast in the Cave," nature strips a man of everything that makes him human—not through malice, but through entropy.

The story also marks an early example of Lovecraft's fascination with the boundaries of perception. The narrator, cut off from sight, must rely on sound and instinct to navigate the cave. His senses begin to deceive him, and his imagination fills in the blanks with nightmare. But in the end, it is not a hallucination that threatens him—it is reality. And this reversal is key to Lovecraft's aesthetic: the idea that the most horrifying truths are not those invented by the mind, but those revealed when the mind is stripped of its illusions.

In this way, "The Beast in the Cave" functions as a kind of fable—a story with a moral, though not a comforting one. It warns us that civilization is a surface condition, maintained by light, order, and community. Take those away, and the human form, both physical and psychological, begins to dissolve. We are not above the animal. We are not immune to transformation. We are, at best, temporary.

This modern edition has been carefully updated to retain Lovecraft's early narrative structure while refining the language for clarity and flow. Archaic turns of phrase have been gently modernized, and sentence constructions have been smoothed to ensure accessibility without compromising tone or atmosphere. The result is a version of the story that remains faithful to the original while allowing its themes to resonate more powerfully with contemporary readers.

To read "The Beast in the Cave" is to experience the essential Lovecraftian question: What is the cost of confronting the unknown? In this story, the unknown is not the stars, the deep sea, or the outer limits of time—it is a cave, a darkness, and the horrifying realization that the monster may not be something we find, but something we become. It is an introduction not only to Lovecraft's imagination, but to the philosophical core of his entire worldview: that identity is fragile, perception is flawed, and horror begins the moment we see ourselves clearly.

The Beast in the Cave

The terrible truth that had slowly been creeping into my mind was now clear: I was completely, hopelessly lost in the huge, winding depths of Mammoth Cave. No matter which way I turned, I couldn't find anything familiar to guide me back. I had to face the fact that I would never again see sunlight or the peaceful hills and valleys of the outside world. Hope was gone. Still, because I had studied philosophy all my life, I felt a strange kind of calm in how I handled the situation. I had read stories about people going mad in situations like this, but I didn't panic. Once I understood I was truly lost, I stayed quiet and composed.

Even the idea that I might have wandered far beyond the reach of any rescue party didn't shake me. If I had to die, I thought, then at least this grand and mysterious cave was a resting place just as good— maybe even better—than a grave in some cemetery. This thought gave me more peace than fear.

I was sure I would eventually die from starvation. Some people had gone insane in similar situations, but I felt sure that wouldn't happen to me. My mistake was entirely my own. Without telling the guide, I had left the group of tourists and wandered off into areas we weren't supposed to explore. After more than an hour of wandering, I couldn't remember how to get back through the twists and turns I had taken.

My torch was already beginning to fade. Soon, I would be surrounded by total, nearly physical darkness deep underground. As the dim, flickering light weakened, I found myself wondering how exactly my end would come. I remembered hearing about a group of people with lung disease who had once lived in this massive cave, hoping its steady temperature and fresh air would heal them. Instead, they died in strange and horrible ways. I had passed their crumbling old huts earlier with the tour group and had wondered what would happen to someone healthy who stayed in the cave too long. Now, it looked like I might find out— unless hunger took me first.

When the last weak flickers of my torch faded into darkness, I promised myself I'd try everything to escape. I took a deep breath and shouted as loudly as I could, hoping my cries might reach the guide. But deep down, I didn't think anyone would hear me. My voice just echoed back from the cave walls, seeming to fill the whole black maze without ever finding another ear.

Then, all of a sudden, I froze. I thought I heard soft footsteps coming toward me over the rocky ground. Could I be rescued so soon? Maybe the guide had noticed I was missing and followed my trail into the cave. I felt a wave of hope and was about to call out again—when my joy turned to fear.

The sound I heard wasn't right. In the deep silence of the cave, the guide's boots should have echoed loudly. But these steps were soft and quiet, like something walking with padded feet—like a cat. And when I listened closely, it seemed like there were four footsteps instead of two.

I suddenly believed that my shouting had attracted a wild animal, maybe a mountain lion that had somehow wandered into the cave. Maybe, I thought grimly, this was a quicker and kinder death than slowly starving. Still, my survival instincts kicked in. Even if escaping the beast only bought me more time before dying, I was determined not to give up easily.

I found myself assuming the creature meant harm. Hoping it would pass me by, I stayed as silent as possible. Maybe, without any sound to follow, it would lose track of me like I had lost my way. But that hope was short-lived. The soft steps kept getting closer. I realized the animal must have caught my scent—which, in the cave's still, clean air, could probably be followed from far away.

Realizing I had to protect myself from something strange and unseen in the dark, I gathered the largest pieces of rock I could find scattered around the cave floor. I held one in each hand, ready to use them, and waited quietly for whatever was coming. The creepy sound of paws tapping the ground grew closer. The way the creature moved was odd—it mostly walked on all fours, but sometimes I thought it used only two legs.

I began to wonder what kind of animal it might be. Maybe it was a poor creature that had wandered into the cave long ago and gotten trapped, surviving off blind fish, bats, and rats. It might have even eaten regular fish carried in by floodwaters from Green River, which somehow connected to the cave.

As I waited in the darkness, I imagined what changes cave life could have caused to the creature's body. I thought about the terrible stories of people who had once lived in the cave to treat their illnesses and ended up dying in horrifying ways. Then it hit me—even if I managed to kill the thing, I wouldn't be able to see what it looked like. My torch had gone out long ago, and I had no matches.

The pressure on my mind was intense. My imagination ran wild, filling the darkness around me with terrifying shapes that felt like they were closing in. The footsteps came even closer. I felt frozen in place, too scared to scream. My arm felt too heavy to throw the rock when the time came.

Now the footsteps were almost right next to me. I could hear the creature breathing hard, like it had come from far away and was tired. Suddenly, I broke out of my frozen state. Aiming carefully with my ears, I threw one of the rocks toward the sound. It hit close—I heard the thing jump and land a short distance away, then stop.

I threw the second rock. This time, I hit it. I could tell by the sound that it had collapsed to the ground and wasn't moving. Overcome with relief, I leaned against the wall, breathing heavily. I could still hear the creature breathing—it was hurt, but not dead. I no longer wanted to get close or finish it off. Some deep, irrational fear held me back. Instead, I ran in what I thought was the direction I had come from, not caring where I ended up.

Then I heard something else—a series of quick, sharp clicks. Within seconds, I recognized the sound: it was the guide! I screamed in joy as I saw the faint flicker of a torchlight above. I ran toward it, and before I knew it, I was lying on the ground, clutching the guide's boots, babbling nonsense, crying with relief, and pouring out my story.

When I calmed down, the guide told me that he'd realized I was missing when the group reached the cave entrance. Using his own sense of direction, he'd searched the nearby tunnels and found me after four hours.

Once I had recovered a bit, I felt brave enough—now that I wasn't alone—to go back and see what I had hit. We walked back to the spot, and soon we saw a white shape on the cave floor. It was whiter than even the pale limestone.

We crept closer and gasped. It was the strangest creature either of us had ever seen. It looked like a large ape, maybe one that had escaped from a traveling circus. Its fur was snow-white, likely from years in the dark cave, and there wasn't much of it—except on its head, where it grew long and thick, falling over its shoulders. The creature was lying face-down, its arms and legs bent in an odd way, which explained why it had sometimes walked on two legs and other times on four. Its fingers and toes had long, claw-like nails, and its hands and feet didn't seem to grip things well—probably from living so long in this dark place. It had no tail.

The breathing was now weak. The guide pulled out his pistol, planning to end its suffering. But then the creature made a strange noise that stopped him. It wasn't a normal animal sound. It was deep and broken, like it came from something that hadn't made a sound in a very long time. The noise continued faintly.

Suddenly, a final burst of energy ran through its body. It twitched, and then rolled over onto its back. For a moment, I was frozen in horror by what I saw. Its eyes—deep, empty, jet-black—were surrounded by pale white skin and fur. They looked like they belonged to something that had lived in darkness forever. But the face itself wasn't like an ape's. It was less animal-like, more human. And it had a real nose.

As we stared at the creature in shock, its lips moved, and a few sounds came out. Then it died.

The guide grabbed my arm, shaking so badly that his torchlight flickered, casting eerie shadows all around us.

I didn't move. I just stared, frozen with horror.

But soon the fear faded, replaced by awe, sadness, and a strange kind of respect. The sounds the creature had made just before dying told us the awful truth.

The thing I had hit—the strange creature in the dark cave—was, or had once been, a man.

THE END

Thank You for Reading

Dear Reader,

We hope this timeless classic has sparked your imagination and enriched your literary journey. Now that you've turned the final page, we want to share a vision for the future of reading—one where every classic you've ever wanted to explore is at your fingertips, in a format that best suits your life.

We'd like to invite you to gain immediate, unlimited digital & audiobook access to hundreds of the most treasured literary classics ever written—along with the option to secure deluxe paperback, hardcover & box set editions at printing cost. Together, we can spark a new global literary renaissance alongside our small, independent publishing house called "The Library of Alexandria."

Thousands of years ago, the Library of Alexandria stood as a beacon of knowledge—until it was lost to history. We aim to reignite that spirit of preservation and discovery right now, in the modern age—only this time, it's accessible to all, in every language and every format.

Picture a world where every timeless classic, novel, poem, or philosophical treatise is not only available to read but also updated for today's readers—modernized, translated into any language or dialect, and ready to enjoy in any format you choose, whether that is in an eBook, audiobook, paperback, or deluxe hardcover & box set version a printing cost.

By joining our movement to rebuild the modern Library of Alexandria, you become part of an unprecedented mission to offer:

- **Unlimited Audiobook & eBook Access** to the **Greatest Classics of All Time**

  Instantly explore thousands of legendary works, from Plato and Shakespeare to Jane Austen and Leo Tolstoy. All are instantly ready to read or listen to, giving you a complete literary universe at your fingertips.

- **Paperback & Deluxe Editions at Printing Costs:**

  Purchase any title in a paperback, deluxe hardbound, or deluxe boxset edition at printing costs, shipped right to your doorstep. Curate your personal library of Alexandria with editions worthy of display— crafted to last, designed to captivate, and delivered straight to your door.

- **Modern translations for Contemporary Readers in all languages and dialects**

  Discover a vast selection of classics reimagined in clear, current language—no more struggling with outdated phrases or obscure references. Next to the original versions, we aim to offer translations in as many languages and dialects as possible.

  As we continue our translation efforts and add new languages, readers everywhere can connect with these works as if they were written today. By bridging linguistic divides, you're contributing to ensuring that these timeless stories become more meaningful, accessible, and inspiring for people across the globe.

- **Your Personal Library of Alexandria:**

  Over the months and years, you'll curate a unique physical archive of classics—each volume a testament to your taste, curiosity, and love of knowledge. It's not just about owning books—it's about curating a cultural legacy you'll cherish and pass down for generations to come.

- **Join a Global Literary Renaissance:**

  Your support fuels an ongoing mission: allowing us to reinvest in offering deluxe print editions (including special boxsets) at their true cost, broaden the range of available formats and translations, and extend the reach of these works to new audiences worldwide. By joining today, you're not just preserving a legacy of masterpieces; you set in motion a powerful wave of literary accessibility.

We are more than a publisher—we're a movement, and we can't do it alone. Your support lets us scale our mission, preserving and reimagining history's greatest works for tomorrow's readers.

Become a Torchbearer of knowledge.

Thank you for picking up this book and allowing us into your literary journey. As you turn the pages, know that you're part of something larger: a global effort to keep these stories alive, share their wisdom across borders and generations, and spark a true cultural revival for the modern era.

If this resonates with you—please consider taking the next step by visiting:

www.libraryofalexandria.com

With gratitude and a shared love of knowledge,

The Modern Library of Alexandria Team

Visit:

www.libraryofalexandria.com

Or scan the code below: